The Driving Test

PRAISE FOR *STORYSHARES*

"One of the brightest innovators and game-changers in the education industry."
– Forbes

"Your success in applying research-validated practices to promote literacy serves as a valuable model for other organizations seeking to create evidence-based literacy programs."
- Library of Congress

"We need powerful social and educational innovation, and Storyshares is breaking new ground. The organization addresses critical problems facing our students and teachers. I am excited about the strategies it brings to the collective work of making sure every student has an equal chance in life."
– Teach For America

"Around the world, this is one of the up-and-coming trailblazers changing the landscape of literacy and education."
- International Literacy Association

"It's the perfect idea. There's really nothing like this. I mean wow, this will be a wonderful experience for young people."   - Andrea Davis Pinkney, Executive Director, Scholastic

"Reading for meaning opens opportunities for a lifetime of learning. Providing emerging readers with engaging texts that are designed to offer both challenges and support for each individual will improve their lives for years to come. Storyshares is a wonderful start."
- David Rose, Co-founder of CAST & UDL

The Driving Test

Monique Hayes

STORYSHARES

Story Share, Inc.
New York. Boston. Philadelphia.

Published in the United States by Story Share, Inc.

The characters and events in this book are fictitious. Any similarity to real persons, living or dead, is entirely coincidental.

Storyshares
Story Share, Inc.
24 N. Bryn Mawr Avenue #340
Bryn Mawr, PA 19010-3304
www.storyshares.org

Inspiring reading with a new kind of book.

Interest Level: High School
Grade Level Equivalent: 4.1

9798885979863

Book design by Storyshares

Printed in the United States of America

Storyshares Presents

1

Enrique is unaccompanied as the long line inches forward. The tear in his sweat-soaked shirt is visible. But his pants are pressed as nicely as possible.

His dark hair never needed much attention because a flick would do the trick. His mother made him comb it every day, anyway. She swore the neighbors would talk.

The Driving Test

2

He would say that his mother had raised his sister Anita to be the family's accomplishment. She sailed through second grade.

After skipping two more, she was shorter than her classmates. She announced she would not skip any more.

Now, she's firmly set in ninth grade. Her five-year-old bookbag is nearly falling apart.

When Anita was barely above his knees, she was writing her name in the dirt of their backyard. She dotted the *i* with authority.

Then, the book fairs would come. The boxes parked on the living room floor made it known.

His sister would show him her treasures later. This space, in between her return from school and his return from work was reserved for her and her books.

The authors definitely made a great first impression. She swore her allegiances.

No one was more cunning than Mark Twain. Or more adventurous than Rudyard Kipling. And *no one* was more bewitching than Emily Brontë.

These were only names on book spines to him. All he saw were surnames slanted to fit the book's curves.

3

Enrique moves slightly to the side so that a father can push a double stroller past him. The infant twins are crying in alarm because of the foreignness of this place.

He remembers feeling foreign when his father took him to the field. It was so long ago.

He taught Enrique to interact with the smallest and shyest of creatures. They peered at ladybugs chewing in the shadows of the stalks.

Field mice greeted them with long, suspicious gazes. Finally, the mice would run off to less crowded territory.

His father was gentle with them as they plucked produce, letting them scamper, crawl, fly away.

When Enrique saw them, he wondered about Anita's animal encounters. Her fair fingers found the most magical creatures on pages...

An inspiring pig made newsworthy by a hardworking spider called Charlotte.

An anxious rabbit that led Alice to hidden places.

Centaurs and talking beavers when you stepped into a wardrobe.

Some days, he touches the branches of sun-lit plants. He rests his hands there as dawn creeps up on his bent shoulders.

Once, his left palm held onto droplets of dew a bit longer. An earthworm curled in his dark hand.

4

The line is getting shorter. There are four people ahead of him—two men in business suits, and a mother and her son.

She's telling him when to renew his license. Assuming he gets it today. The son says he knows. He is beaming with pride.

Enrique's knowledge was gathered while he gathered the gifts of carefully tended fields. He could tell when a rind was ripe by its waxy sheen.

Or he could scratch the skin with his thumbnail. A watermelon was ready if he tapped and heard the hollow thump from within.

He memorized the mating call of birds vacationing in the trees during the harvest. His father let him figure it out on his own.

He called them the quiet, natural lessons of life. Enrique thought about how long these lessons would last. Would they be longer than Anita's?

He's not sure so he whispers them to himself to remember them when he works alone.

5

On their first day out in the field, the wheat shifted. The black crows were calm.

The wheat stalks looked like golden feathers dancing, the way the wind moved them back and forth.

As he and his father moved from row to row, Enrique could see the blend of colors more easily. The wheat started off as a deep, rich yellow, then bled to a topaz, then a comely tan.

His father said that even though they'd be working primarily with fruit, Enrique's first experience should be in a ground of gold.

His father mowed with the crop shredder. It sounded like thousands of tiny, moving scissors. Enrique lay at the edge of the scene, listening and watching.

He saw the gold fall on the grass, tickling his calves and hovering over his nose. His eyes strayed to the road.

The winding asphalt stretched farther and farther. He always knew when a car coming because the asphalt would seem to growl like a churning river.

The only thing left for him to do was to guess what was going to come.

Was it a clunker, retrieved from the scrap yard, that rattled when it went by?

Was it a reliable school bus that carried his childhood neighbors?

Was it a van, packed for a purpose?

Sometimes it was the last guess. That's when he closed his brown eyes to the sun and remembered.

6

The van was hot. Enrique had to be bribed by a lollipop from his mother so he'd stop crying.

Anita sat in their father's lap, clutching his collar. Her sunflower barrettes resembled weeds in the darkness.

Enrique held out his hand in the warm air to the six passengers across from them. His mother automatically slapped it away.

The oldest man smiled. Two of his front teeth were missing.

All their faces were papery. They looked at peace,

expressions with many lines on their skin. Squiggles of serenity.

Right then, Enrique suspected they had a story to tell. They would tell their children about the crossing.

Their children, younger than Enrique, would wonder about the cramped space, the hopeful and serious silence, the fading guilt.

Children would weigh their lives against it. Maybe, like Enrique, they would look at the road to remember.

Or maybe they would remember the passage from Mexico as a moment that has disappeared in the twinkling of a tear and turn away.

Enrique chose to hold the story, because he didn't possess many others.

7

The mother in front of him sighs deeply. "Remember, driving is..."

"A responsibility," finishes her son. "I'm a different driver than Dad, Mom. I'm careful."

Enrique stares at the mother. She is biting her lip, nervous and worried. The son whistles as they walk to the woman at the main desk.

"Hello," says the mother. "We're here for the driving test."

"Road or written test? Or both?" says the woman.

"Both," replies the mother.

The woman at the desk shifts some papers. Enrique fixes his gaze on a rolling pencil that the boy catches before it finds the floor.

The boy twirls the pencil as the woman locates the forms.

Enrique only twirled his when he was nervous. The standardized test brought on continual twirling.

8

He was a good copier. Drawing letters or tracing shapes kept his pencil from twirling through kindergarten, first, and second grade.

Then, the test. The standardized exam that crammed every word possible into the test packet. It came along to make him twirl.

Minutes went by and he squirmed in his seat. His eyes teared up at the elegantly presented paragraphs and multiple-choice questions.

A word seemed like one thing but was completely something else. His brain stuttered the words he should've been able to comprehend.

He knew this wouldn't be the last of these tests. Setting his head down, he dreamed imaginary words that he'd know and no one else would.

9

His counselor summoned Enrique and his parents to discuss the empty test.

Why are there no marks, the counselor asked. Not a single one.

Did he have a pencil? Is he lazy?

Enrique thought of the excuses in his mind, next to the imaginary words. When asked, Enrique simply said, *the words I liked weren't on there*.

His mother offered an apology for his stubbornness. His father stroked his beard. The counselor suggested a tutor and another meeting.

10

The three of them went home to discuss the problem further.

Enrique wrapped his arms around his blue, wool winter coat as they sat on the couch. He wanted to shield himself from any looks of shame.

The defense was unnecessary. His father stared at him longingly, lovingly.

He set a cool hand on Enrique's small arm. He asked if Enrique could read.

"I don't know," answered Enrique, staring at his coat.

"Have you tried?"

"Yes."

His mother choked back a sob.

"If the tests are too hard, he will follow me," said his father. "He can always learn to read later like we did."

Other choices weren't available to them at the time. The fields needed more hands, especially fresh ones.

Gratitude wouldn't pay the tutor. His mother understood.

She took a literacy class in her late twenties, following Anita's birth. She just thought her children might learn earlier than she did.

Still, Enrique was eight and eager. He could become a fine man, like his father.

"Just fine," guaranteed his father.

Enrique rested his head on his father's lap.

11

Bright flashes glow to Enrique's right. He sees a young woman, with skull earrings. She is seated on a stool grinning for her first license photo.

The legs of her jeans touch the floor. The earrings jangle like tossed seeds splattering on leaves.

Whenever the clunkers came down the road, Enrique would pound his pocket and hears the jangle of coins through the field. It was his ritual. It assures him he has money. His own money.

He can already afford this, he reassures himself. He can

already afford that.

His ritual of doing a private inventory of attainable items is getting tiring. He pounds his pocket now, waiting for his turn at the counter.

Currently, he'd like a Miata because they're cool. And his cousin drove one.

His father said that as long as he was practical about it, he would give Enrique a little help. Then he could buy a car.

Enrique assumed this promise was because his life had very few joys in it.

There were no girls under the scorching heat of the day. If they came, they would see their boyfriends at school tomorrow.

Every field trip Enrique had been on was to the field.

His friends were friends on weekends. Often, he'd sleep away those hours. When that happened, he would miss his friends and the energy that buzzed in his small town.

A car could wake him up, though. That's because a car meant something.

It meant there were places beyond the road for him to see. People beyond the state line who could be waiting to meet him.

12

"Go to room 5B," instructs the woman, handing the test to the son.

The mother and son exchange an awkward hug before he disappears into a room near a water cooler.

"They grow up fast, don't they?" says the mother to the woman.

"That they do," says the woman.

The Driving Test

13

Anita's first book report was about four women who were growing up. They braved the Massachusetts cold in tight clothes, while their father was away at war.

Anita explained the plot of the spirited, brave sisters in their living room. She wanted to practice on a kind audience.

The sisters found work, wrote, and fell in love. Enrique listened intently.

He finally had to ask why the boys weren't featured as

much. Anita called him silly and told him the book was called *Little Women*, and that was all there was to it.

Enrique stayed quiet until "the end" was announced. While their parents heaped praise on Anita's efforts, he went to the kitchen.

He lay against the refrigerator and heard the hum of the appliance. Enrique hit it as his lips trembled.

Ice toppled inside. He pictured the Himalayan mountains, white and steep.

The fridge gurgled, and the floor shook for a few seconds. It made him think of a magic carpet ride.

There were no maps to get to the snow-capped mountains. The image was intimidating enough for him to find it.

There were no instructions to make the carpet fly. It flew in the fury of his silent disappointment.

14

"Do you speak English?" says a voice.

The woman at the front desk is the speaker of the question. She has an ugly brooch, some cheap pin, holding together her poorly constructed shawl.

Enrique nods and clutches his wallet. The wallet is worn at the edges, but still keeps his money as best it can.

"I would like to sign up for driver's education," says Enrique.

"Then you'll need a list of area driving schools," says the woman, doing another search for this document.

Opening his wallet, he folds back the bills to get to a tiny scrap of paper that has what he needs. Anita had cut out and circled the best driving school in their town for him.

"I have the one I want," says Enrique.

The woman stares at him skeptically but reads the name.

"That school is only operating during the summer from now on," says the woman. "Here. Read this list and pick another one."

15

Enrique puts his hand against it, steadying the paper as if it would make it easier. His mouth starts to open.

This has become a regular occurrence when signs suddenly spring up at the discount stores, new products appear on the job, or cars he doesn't recognize are be listed in the classifieds.

He'd sound it out until he got pretty close. Enrique turns the list to the left and then to the right. The words blur with each movement.

He picks up a pencil to pass some time. The words still remain black, concrete. They are hidden from the hope that rests in his heart.

He knows cars very well. It's a language he was surrounded by for years, listening to the farmers and the mechanics at work. It isn't a hard vocabulary since he loves the topic.

He convinced himself that most of the terms he knows would be on the written test. His cousin passed with flying colors.

Things would be different in this situation. They had to be. Reading wouldn't stop this rite of passage.

"Is there a problem, sweetie?" says the woman, her brooch seeming to get bigger as she takes a heavy breath.

He lets his lips meet once more. No, he doesn't want the illusion to drop. There are ways to make things seem similar.

Enrique could be the same as other kids.

16

Anita came to the fields when they were smaller. She wore colorful dresses the shades of spring flowers.

She didn't know how to plant bulbs, so he showed her. Their hands wrapped around the bulb together as they lowered it into the dirt.

Afterwards, they blew bubbles and walked sideways through the rows of tomatoes. Anita blew the biggest bubble Enrique had ever seen. Then he blew a bigger one.

Anita wasn't impressed. She kept trying to outdo him with her exhausted cheeks.

When the bubble came, it was almost the size of his head.

Enrique had no more air to give.

Anita said she saw a bubble just like it in a painting in one of her books. That's when Enrique yelled "so what," punched the bubble, and made her cry.

She cried until they got home. Enrique stared at her red face until their father put her to bed.

He went into her room an hour later and flipped through each book. When he finally found it—the book with the bubble picture—it had no words.

Enrique kissed her smooth forehead as she rolled in bed. He took the book with him.

In his bedroom, his own tears hit the page on the stunning picture of the giant bubble. He stared at it all night.

17

"I'll take it home and decide," says Enrique.

"All right, but those classes fill up fast," says the woman. "I can give you a driver's handbook, too, for seven dollars."

"No, that's okay," says Enrique.

He stares at the crisp, square pages of the handbook. The cover looks deceptively simple. Like everything else with words.

"Thank you," says Enrique, walking away.

He stops at the entrance.

The same girl who had her picture taken is celebrating with a friend. Their shrieks are piercing and young.

The camera is at ease. It will capture another kid, another day.

Enrique removes his cell phone and calls her.

"Hello?" says his mother.

"Mom," says Enrique. "I'd like to go to a literacy class like you went to, if that's all right."

Her reply is rich and doesn't have too many words. Enrique smiles at the lack of them.

"More than all right."

About The Author

Monique Hayes received her MFA from the University of Maryland College Park. Her work appears in *Midway Journal*, *Prick of the Spindle*, *From the Depths*, *Touch: The Journal of Healing*, *Mused*, *Birmingham Arts Journal*, among others. She was awarded a 2015 Writers Residency from Wildacres Retreat.

About The Publisher

Story Shares is a nonprofit focused on supporting the millions of teens and adults who struggle with reading by creating a new shelf in the library specifically for them. The ever-growing collection features content that is compelling and culturally relevant for teens and adults, yet still readable at a range of lower reading levels.

Story Shares generates content by engaging deeply with writers, bringing together a community to create this new kind of book. With more intriguing and approachable stories to choose from, the teens and adults who have fallen behind are improving their skills and beginning to discover the joy of reading. For more information, visit storyshares.org.

Easy to Read. Hard to Put Down.